Acting Edition

Wild Horses

by Allison Gregory

SAMUEL FRENCH

ISBN 978-0-573-71055-1

www.concordtheatricals.com
www.concordtheatricals.co.uk

FOR PRODUCTION INQUIRIES

UNITED STATES AND CANADA
info@concordtheatricals.com
1-866-979-0447

UNITED KINGDOM AND EUROPE
licensing@concordtheatricals.co.uk
020-7054-7298

Each title is subject to availability from Concord Theatricals Corp.,
depending upon country of performance. Please be aware that WILD
HORSES may not be licensed by Concord Theatricals Corp. in your
territory. Professional and amateur producers should contact the
nearest Concord Theatricals Corp. office or licensing partner to verify
availability.

This work is published by Samuel French, an imprint of Concord
Theatricals Corp.

No one shall make any changes in this title(s) for the purpose of production. No part of this book may be reproduced, stored in a retrieval system, scanned, uploaded, or transmitted in any form, by any means, now known or yet to be invented, including mechanical, electronic, digital, photocopying, recording, videotaping, or otherwise, without the prior written permission of the publisher. No one shall share this title(s), or any part of this title(s), through any social media or file hosting websites.

For all inquiries regarding motion picture, television, online/digital and other media rights, please contact Concord Theatricals Corp.

MUSIC AND THIRD-PARTY MATERIALS USE NOTE

Licensees are solely responsible for obtaining formal written permission from copyright owners to use copyrighted music and/or other copyrighted third-party materials (e.g. artworks, logos) in the performance of this play and are strongly cautioned to do so. If no such permission is obtained by the licensee, then the licensee must use only original music and materials that the licensee owns and controls. Licensees are solely responsible and liable for clearances of all third-party copyrighted materials, including without limitation music, and shall indemnify the copyright owners of the play(s) and their licensing agent, Concord Theatricals Corp., against any costs, expenses, losses and liabilities arising from the use of such copyrighted third-party materials by licensees. For music, please contact the appropriate music licensing authority in your territory for the rights to any incidental music.

IMPORTANT BILLING AND CREDIT REQUIREMENTS

If you have obtained performance rights to this title, please refer to your licensing agreement for important billing and credit requirements.

WILD HORSES made its world premiere through the National New Play Network (NNPN) at the following theaters: Contemporary American Theatre Festival (CATF), Shepherdstown WVA; New Jersey Repertory Theatre, Long Branch, NJ; Vortex Theatre, Austin, TX; CenterStage Theatre @JCC, Rochester, NY; Subsequent productions include Intiman Theatre in Seattle, WA; Merrimack Repertory Theatre in Lowell, MA; Williamston Theatre in Williamston, MI; Phoenix Theatre in Indianapolis, IN. For the Contemporary American Theatre Festival (CATF) production, the Director was Courtney Sale, Assistant Director Joshua Midgett, Set & Costume Designer Jesse Dreikosen, Lighting Designer John Ambrosone, Sound Designer David Remedios, Stage Manager Samantha Cotton. The cast was as follows:

THE WOMAN . . . . Kate Udall

CHARACTERS

THE WOMAN – 40–60, the mother of teens.

SETTING

The location of this play is a place where people gather: a casual, communal hub. It might be open-mic night at a bar, it could be an open-air food court, or a community center rec-room – or the very theatre we're in.

It was once, in the way back, a Tastee Freeze. Somehow we should know/ sense this.

TIME

Tonight.

AUTHOR'S NOTE

Music should be considered a driving force in this play, use it aggressively to elevate, impel, power the story forward.

The song titles I've listed are what I listened to when I was writing; if you choose to use these songs for your production it is the responsibility of the theatre to obtain specific rights to the music and lyrics (see music note on page iii. Otherwise, use these listed songs as a map to the ambition of each scene, for emotional or tonal shifts in the play, and as a jumping-off-point for original sound design. The music isn't simply incidental; it isn't merely transitional; it should feel essential, and it should be used avidly and generously.

ACKNOWLEDGMENTS

Special thanks to Ed Herendeen, Courtney Sale, Joel Stone, and Rudy Ramirez.

MUSIC

#1: "Horse With No Name" – America

#2: "Living In The Past" – Jethro Tull

#3: "Reelin' In The Years" – Steely Dan

#4: "The Cisco Kid" – War

#5: "I Gotcha" – Joe Tex

#6: "Barracuda" – Heart

#7: "Rock On" – David Essex

#8: "The Rapper" – The Jaggerz

#9: "Me and Mrs. Jones" – Billy Paul

#10: "Don't Let The Sun Go Down On Me" – Elton John

#11: "Smoke On The Water" – Deep Purple

#12: "Superstition" – Stevie Wonder

#13: "Brand New Key" – Melanie

#14: "Black Dog" – Led Zepplin

#15: "Midnight At The Oasis" – Maria Muldaur

#16: "Dancing In The Moonlight" – King Harvest

#17: "Shambala" – Three-Dog Night

#18: "Horse With No Name" – America

#19: "Magic Man" – Heart

#20: "Radar Love" – Golden Earring

#21: "Brand New Key" – Melanie

#22: "Immigrant Song" – Led Zeppelin

#23: "Let's Get It On" – Marvin Gaye

#24: "La Grange" – ZZ Top

#25: "Horse With No Name" – America

#26: "Wild Horses" – The Rolling Stones

"Against all this, Youth,
Flaming like the wild roses,
Flashing like a star out of the twilight;
Its fierce necessity,
Its sharp desire,
Singing and singing."

Prairie Spring by Willa Cather

(The ambient buzz of conversation, a communal space, inside or out, people gathered for a good time.)

(THE WOMAN *enters or is already there. She talks to us, picking up a story she lived to tell. All the characters have names and they are all voiced by* **THE WOMAN.***)*

THE WOMAN. The worst part of The Belt was the waiting
You had to go into their bedroom
your own parents' bedroom
which was awkward
because it's a mysterious room that you really don't
want to think too much about
Get The Belt out of Dad's belt drawer
Lay it on the bed
Pull your pants down
And "think about what you did."
Only just then I couldn't get past thinking about
how much it was going to hurt.
What made it even worse
I kept thinking about Garff Garrett on the waterbed
with his pants around his ankles and his droopy
checkered boxers and Zabby holding a knife
But you don't know that part.

I would *never* tell my kids this. They think I'm at my
book club. I'm not in a book club.

(She hears music [1]. The song.)

Everyday that song played on the radio. That summer
there was a contest and I was going to win it. Whoever
came up with the best name for the horse that didn't
have a name would win, no lie, *a horse.*

You had to send a name in on a postcard, one name
per postcard.
I stamped and pre-addressed ninety postcards.
I was going to win that horse.

We knew all the words by heart.
Every day that summer I sent in a new name for the
horse with no name.
Nobody even knows what the words were supposed to
mean
But still we sang the song
It was our anthem – if we'd known what an anthem
was
It's the thing we sang before doing it
It being the thing we wouldn't be doing if the three of
us weren't together.
Zabby, and Skinny Lynny, and me
Vying testing erupting
Egging each other on to greatness
To infamy
To getting our asses kicked.
Like sneaking into Zabby's parents' pub
They actually had a pub inside their house
Making drinks out of whatever's open
Didn't matter
Jack Daniels, Strawberry Hill, Peppermint Schnapps,
Gin
Doesn't matter because we're thirteen
we hate the taste of all that shit
But we're thirteen
Yeah!

    (Music [2].)

So we pour it all together
The brown and the red and the clear stuff that makes
my nose sting and my eyes water – plus some orange
juice, for body

We pour it all into an empty tennis ball can
And we drink
Holding our noses
It's awful, godawful
But taste is not the point
Taste is the last thing we care about.

I was a good girl
An outstanding student
the perfect child of miserable parents
Corruption fodder
What class do you have right now Zabby says

THE GIRL. Um French.

ZABBY. You're going to be late to your French class.

I'm never late, I say.

ZABBY. Today you're going to be late.

Everybody knew her
Abbey Zilker – Zabby. She was newly notorious
A fist fight with Tonya Yonkers on the bus had gotten
her suspended for three days.
Even though she had a red bald patch where Tonya
yanked a bunch of her dirty blonde hair out it was
pretty much agreed that Zabby won.
Tonya crying
Nobody really concerned because she's a bossy cry
baby.
Now Zabby is back at school
Talking to me
I'm terrified and sort of honored.

ZABBY. You better hurry. You're going to be late to
French.

THE GIRL. Can you, um, would you please give me
back my French book?

(The sound of the late bell.)

ZABBY. Uh oh. Was that the *bell*?

THE GIRL. Oh my god give me my book!

ZABBY. I guess you're late, huh? What are you going to do?

THE GIRL. You're late too, idiot!

ZABBY. So what?

THE GIRL. So we're going to get in trouble! If you get three tardies you get a detention and one more after that you get suspended and after three suspensions you get *expelled*.

ZABBY. How many tardies have you had Frenchy?

None, I say.

ZABBY. I've had *five*.

THE GIRL. Five?

ZABBY. *This week*.

THE GIRL. You could get *expelled*.

ZABBY. *(Sarcastic.) Oh no really?*

THE GIRL. Just shut up and give me my French book please.

ZABBY. Oh look, it's the Assistant Principal.

THE GIRL. Don't let him see us!

ZABBY. How's it going Mr. Miser?

THE GIRL. *(Fierce whisper.)* Oh my god shut up shut up shut up.

ZABBY. Hey sorry Mr. Miser, I meant to bring you raisins today but my rabbit died so no more raisins.

We spent the rest of the afternoon sitting in the Assistant Principal's office.

(Music [3].)

Zabby was everything I was afraid to be
Irreverent, outrageous, attractive, funny
She could even dance like she was black.*
That sounds bad.
You have to remember this was a time when all the
white people were doing disco and we all looked even
whiter.
Zabby was an influence.

> (*If **THE WOMAN** *is a person of color please
> use the following dialogue:*)

Zabby was everything I was afraid to be
Irreverent, outrageous, attractive, funny
And she could *dance.*
Zabby was an influence.

SKINNY LYNNY. Hey Zabby, what if your parents find
out?

That's Skinny Lynny
We're in Zabby's parents' pub making a carafe of our
disgusting magical elixir

ZABBY. They don't care they're at a party.

Skinny Lynny is pouring

THE GIRL. Whoa that's way too much of the brown
stuff Lynny.

SKINNY LYNNY. I'll balance it out with more of the
clear.

She just kind of fell into my life,
Skinny Lynny
She literally fell off her bike in front of my house.
The thing about Skinny Lynny
She was totally accident prone.
It's notable how many near-death encounters she
survived

Some kind of miracle she didn't die sooner
She was just funny that way.

SKINNY LYNNY. Yum, down the hatch!

>   (**SKINNY LYNNY** *plugs her nose and guzzles, gasps, chokes.*)

THE GIRL. Is it bad?

SKINNY LYNNY. Really bad, have some.

>   (*Music [4].*)

Zabby wasn't nearly as bad as her brothers Dean and Don-o.
All things considered she was the responsible one of the litter.
Dean, tall, great-looking
Square-jaw, brooding eyes
Twenty-two or nineteen
I don't know but too old to be a kid
And mean
Pain-seeking mean.

>   (*Music [5].*)

One night we hide in the eucalyptus trees bent over the street
Armed with rotten stolen eggs from the Peaker's chicken farm
Go!
Invisible to the unsuspecting car that had the bad fortune to drive under us
Plop!
We expertly drop fetid bombs on windshields and hoods and laugh 'til we wet our pants.

Zabby look who's coming.

Uh oh
Dean's car
His manhood rumbling on the road below us
Mean Dean
We smell glory.

One-two-go go go I shout!
We pelt that macho station wagon with heart-felt
hatred and joy and thirteen-year-old revenge
Bam Bam Bam!

Miscalculation.
It takes him no time to put two and two together

> *(She makes the sound of* **DEAN** *slamming on
> the brakes.)*

> *(Music [6].)*

Dean backing up like a maniac
That car has never moved so fast
Us screaming, laughing, skittering down the tree
Scattering in every direction.
Dean bolting from the passenger side of his car
because the driver door is busted
Dean chasing down his sister
Dean tackling her to the ground, smashing rotten eggs
in her face and hair
Dean grinding bits of shell hard into her head
Dean grunting
Zabby too tough to cry

ZABBY. Get off me you fat-ass fag!

Me and Skinny Lynny tearing out of there
Skinny Lynny of course tripping on a pothole
Scraping up her chin her knees her elbows
I stoop to help her but Dean is coming
Big mean smile
I didn't do it Dean, Lynny lies
Stop it, don't Dean don't!

Dean not stopping
Crushing egg into Skinny Lynny's head, her face
Her hair a matted mess
Her mouth full of dirt
Dean getting up

Looking for me
But I am hell-bent, tearing through someone's
backyard.
Dean yelling

  DEAN. I'm watching you, you bitch, you little bitch.
  I'll teach you to fuck with my car squirt!

He never did catch me that night.
He never did forget.

Saffire
Shiloh
Dark Lady

"I been through the desert on a horse *with* a name?"
It doesn't sound right
But that's how you win the contest

  SKINNY LYNNY. What if it's a boy?

Hitchcock
Elton John
Ringo
Bozo.

  THE GIRL. Everyone will look for the hidden meaning
  in the name.

Destiny
Roulette
Fickle Finger of Fate

We were standing in Garff Garrett's driveway
Me, Zabby, Skinny Lynny, Garff Garrett
And some little cousin of his.
No really the cousin wasn't very tall.

Cousin just stood there with his hands in his pockets
He wasn't show-offy like Garff Garret who was full of it.

The only reason we had walked there was because
Garff Garrett
He said he'd gotten a bunch of weed
Hot shot.
He told Zabby he'd give her some if she came over.

Garff Garrett was always making like his family was
rich.
Whatever, but he lived in a dirty house at the top of a
hill at the end of a winding road.
So we're there and he's talking about nothing
It's obvious he has a hard on for Zabby
Everybody does
Zabby can't stand Garff Garrett
Nobody can
But she's wily.
So we're standing in the driveway not really listening
or caring.

GARFF. Zabby are you going to Jeff Cranover's party?

ZABBY. I don't know, maybe, are you?

He invited me says Garff

Who cares, I thought.

GARFF. Did you go to his last one?

ZABBY. I don't remember.

GARFF. I was invited to that one too.

Sure you were, I thought.

GARFF. I was pretty high I can't remember if I saw
you there.

And I'm thinking because you weren't there because
you weren't invited A-hole.

GARFF. I'm having a big party, like everyone can come you know? I can do anything I want, my parents' don't care. I've just gotta wait 'til they get back.

Your parents are going to be at the party, asks Skinny Lynny.

GARFF. No pinhead, they have to buy the keg.

ZABBY. Where's the pot Garff?

GARFF. Yeah the pot, uh. In my room.

Go and get it Garff says Skinny Lynny.

GARFF. Hey Zabby, ever been on a waterbed?

I think Garff Garrett is a lonely guy.

ZABBY. You have a *waterbed*?

GARFF. Hell yes, California king with a heater. Hot and wet.

Creepy lonely.

GARFF. Come on, I'll show you. What? I'll give you the pot after you look at my waterbed swear to god.

Despite every screaming impulse otherwise we follow Garff Garrett and his "cousin" into his bedroom to look at his waterbed

SKINNY LYNNY. It's Oh-My-God huuuge.

GARFF. See told you, biggest one in the store.

That waterbed was big. At least he didn't lie about that.

GARFF. Come on get on it.

THE GIRL. What's that smell?

Garff Garrett pushes a pile of dirty magazines, french fries, batteries, and a steak knife off the bed.

GARFF. You gotta lay down to get the full experience.

THE GIRL. Whoa. How do you stay on it.

SKINNY LYNNY. It's squishy.

ZABBY. Feels like warm waves.

GARFF. Feels even better with no clothes on.

I'm watching Garff's cousin in case he tries to lock the
door. But he's just leaning against the wall, hands in his
pockets I'm pretty sure he can't actually do anything
else. Why am I paranoid?

GARFF. The best is when you're loaded and naked and
you close your eyes. It's like being on a magic carpet in
the Bahamas. So what do you say, Zabby?

ZABBY. I say we smoke some.

SKINNY LYNNY. Totally smoke some.

GARFF. No way, my parents.

You said your parents are out of town, I say. You said
your parents don't care.

ZABBY. We'll be cool city. Come on Garff, where is it?

SKINNY LYNNY. Where is it Garff?

GARFF. Everyone gets naked first.

Gross no! I say. I'm not getting naked.

GARFF. Shirts off, then.

SKINNY LYNNY. Fuck off Garff.

GARFF. Forget it then, no skin no weed.

We have walked a long way for nothing.
That's when Zabby turns Garff Garret's stereo on.

    (Music [7].)

ZABBY. I like to dance before I strip.

Now
Zabby is a really good dancer
But what the hell is she talking about?
She starts to sway and
And something in Garff clicks

Some kind of switch in his pea brain
She is hypnotizing him!
He doesn't say anything, just takes off his shirt
Starts moving his pale chest and arms and hips
Rolling his lax belly
Like if one of those plastic troll-dolls danced
underwater.
He is standing up on his waterbed gyrating and
undulating with the waves.

> *(**GARFF GARRETT** gyrates and undulates.)*

ZABBY. Give us what we came here for. The pot, Garff.

Garff Garrett doesn't hear or doesn't care
He is undoing his belt
He is unzipping his pants
Pulling them down and leaving them around his
ankles
Assaulting our eyes with his droopy checkered boxers.
Skinny Lynny looks away.

SKINNY LYNNY. Stop Garff.

Just tell us where the stuff is, I say.

GARFF. Don't tell them Dirk!

That's when Cousin Dirk with his hands in his pockets
starts snickering.

ZABBY. You little *shit*. You don't have any!

SKINNY LYNNY. Fucking Garff.

GARFF. Yes I do, I have a whole stash.

ZABBY. You do not, you're a liar.

GARFF. Yes I do, but you're not getting any of it!

Zabby jumps on Garff Garret pinning him on the surging waterbed. I'm starting to wish I hadn't come.

ZABBY. Where is it nickle-dick?

GARFF. Forget it I don't have to give you any.

ZABBY. I came to your house fucker, now are you gonna give me what you said you'd give me, or am I gonna hit you?

GARFF. Hah, make me slut!

Wait
I don't think I remembered to tell you
Zabby was a competitive swimmer
National Junior Olympics champ in the butterfly and the backstroke. All that strength in her shoulders and arms.
So when she punched Garff Garrett in the stomach
I felt sorry for him
Kind of.

GARFF. *(Gasping.)* Crazy ugly whore, now you're really not getting any. Dirk don't tell them where it is.

It's in his asshole, said cousin Dirk.

GARFF. Shut up Dirk!

ZABBY. Guess we'd better check.

GARFF. Hah, no way, you wouldn't you're too chicken.

Skinny Lynny sits on his legs, I sit on his arms.
Zabby starts pulling down his droopy checkered boxers
I close my eyes
I so don't want Garff Garrett's penis to be the first one burned into my memory.
Instead of feeling unpopular at that moment Garff Garrett seems pretty turned on

He's twisting and groaning
The bed is roiling and splashing, tossing us around

  GARFF. What are you going to do to me. Huh? Huh?
Come on.

That's when Zabby picks up the steak knife.

  ZABBY. Turn over, Perv!

Weirdly he does.

  GARFF. Oh yeah what are you gonna do now? Huh?

He closes his eyes *and smiles.*
Cousin Dirk says wait man I think your parents just
rolled in.
Garff Garrett doesn't hear or doesn't care
Zabby grips the knife
She's freaking me out
Even Skinny Lynny is like

        (**SKINNY LYNNY** *makes a freaked out face.*)

Then.
Zabby plunges the knife *into the waterbed.*

At first nothing happens
We're all in shock.
Then she pulls the knife *out* of the waterbed
And all hell breaks loose
Water spouting and spraying the room, Garff spazzing

  GARFF. Get off, get off, get off my waterbed!

It's hard to move quickly on those things

  THE GIRL. Let's get out of here!

We pile out the window above his bed and Skinny
Lynny falls onto the ground on her chin
She's bleeding from her mouth
Luckily she has braces so her teeth stay in.

Garff Garret is still spazzing.

GARFF. They're going to kill me, my fucking parents are fucking going to fucking kill me.

We pick Skinny Lynny up and race out of his yard and gallop halfway home
Finally, finally stopping to breathe

THE GIRL. Oh my god oh my god! Who knows what he would have

ZABBY. The perv

SKINNY LYNNY. Totally

THE GIRL. I gotta get home.

SKINNY LYNNY. What about tonight? Want to get drunk?

My house, says Zabby, my parents will be gone.

Totally.

(*Music [8].*)

Something's in the air
I can feel it when I walk across the threshold into my house
The betrayal.

MOTHER. Did you take something out of my scarf drawer?

THE GIRL. Why are you asking me Mom?

MOTHER. Because your sister

My sister Carrie-Ann, The Favorite, comes in. All I can do is give her the silent killing look.

MOTHER. Your sister said she didn't take it.

THE GIRL. Of course you believe her.

MOTHER. Did you take it?

Take what, I say.

CARRIE-ANN. Mom?

MOTHER. Not now Carrie-Ann.

(*To* **THE GIRL**.)

Why were you digging through my scarf drawer in the first place missy?

THE GIRL. I was looking for a scarf?

MOTHER. Liar. You've never worn a scarf in your entire life.

THE GIRL. Well I was going to *start* but now forget it.

CARRIE-ANN. *Um, Mom?*

MOTHER. Be quiet Carrie-Ann. *What did you do with it?*

THE GIRL. I didn't find one I liked.

MOTHER. *The letter*. Where did you put the letter?

CARRIE-ANN. Mom. Mom. Mom. Mom. Mom.

THE GIRL. What *letter?*

CARRIE-ANN. Can I first say something?

MOTHER. Shut up for once Carrie-Ann!

I didn't take any letter, I say. What's the big deal about it anyway?

MOTHER. Look at me. *Listen to me.* You have no idea, missy. That is my personal property! *My property.*

FATHER. What's going on?

CARRIE-ANN. Dad's home.

Mom, silence.

FATHER. What's all the racket about?

MOTHER. Nothing, it's about nothing.

FATHER. Is she stealing again?

Meaning me.

MOTHER. We've already talked about it.

FATHER. What did you steal this time?

MOTHER. Oh for godssake leave her alone, it's not important.

FATHER. It goddamn is Frida, it is important if she's stealing.

MOTHER. I don't want to talk about this now.

FATHER. When should we talk about it? Next week? Next year? When she's in juvy or jail or we've been sued in court? Because that's where all this is headed.

MOTHER. Stop talking like some kind of jackass.

FATHER. Go to hell.

MOTHER. You go to hell.

THE GIRL. How about I just go?

There she goes
My mother silently melted into a heap on the floor
A cataplectic fit. "Limp man syndrome," not the first time, or the last. It's okay, you get used to it.

> (**FATHER** *steps over incapacitated* **MOTHER** *to address* **THE GIRL**.)

FATHER. Did you or didn't you steal from your mother?

This was a grey area.

> (*Music [9].*)

See The Favorite started having an affair about three months earlier with a guy across the street.
He'd moved back in with his parents

So now they were doing it.

He was twenty-six she was fourteen

Yeah just

Yeah.

She didn't even know he was married until it kind of
slipped out one day like "oh yeah."

No one knew what was up with the wife

Anyway it was disgusting and I told her to stop and
she tried but they were "in love."

THE FAVORITE. You can't tell anyone. Please don't tell
anyone.

THE GIRL. Are you at least using something, birth
control?

Her, silence.

THE GIRL. Oh my god Carrie-Ann.

THE FAVORITE. I don't have money for that.

THE GIRL. What are you thinking? Make *him* pay.

THE FAVORITE.   He's living with his parents, he's
between jobs.

THE GIRL. And he's a jerk, hello. You need to use birth
control so you don't make a little jerk.

THE FAVORITE. He's not a jerk. You can't tell anyone
promise? I'd kill myself if mom and dad found out.

I was pretty sure they'd kill her first.

So when I happened upon an envelope stuffed with
cash in mom's scarf drawer...

What? I was looking for a scarf. Anyway why was she
hiding so much money?

I instinctively took some cash for Carrie-Ann so she
could buy whatever she needed to not have the jerk's
baby.

But, and I swear this, there was no letter in the drawer.

THE GIRL. I didn't steal the letter Dad.

FATHER. What letter?

THE GIRL. There wasn't one!

FATHER. So you're telling me you didn't steal?

THE GIRL. No.

FATHER. No you didn't steal or no you're not telling me that?

THE GIRL. I'm confused.

FATHER. Are you a thief or are you a liar?

ME. I don't know.

FATHER. Get The Belt.

THE GIRL. It's not even fair!

FATHER. Go get The Belt.

THE GIRL. Dad no wait I'm sorry.

FATHER. You should have thought of that before you decided to be a lying thief.

(*Music [10].*)

Like I said
The worst part of The Belt was the waiting
The no pants was pretty humiliating too.
I don't know how I was supposed to learn anything
except how afraid of my father I was in that moment.
So I waited
I tried to not think about Garff Garrett with his pants
around his ankles and his droopy checkered boxers
But I couldn't help it
I didn't know anymore whose shame I was feeling.

After it was over – it seemed like my father was
trying to whip more than just the lying and stealing
out of me. Like his wife's secrets and his daughter's
shape-shifting and his lack of control over any of us –

I didn't cry.
I wasn't going to give him that payoff.

FATHER. You're grounded. Go to your room. Now.

Me, silence
No grimacing, no whimpering
Nothing.
I cried hard into my pillow under the blanket so no
one could hear me
I fell asleep.
When I woke up it was quiet downstairs, dark out.
Mom would be watching repeats
All in the Family, Good Times, Happy Days.

Dad would be in his basement office avoiding Mom.
The Favorite would be having phone sex with her
married boyfriend
Shit.
I couldn't stand it
I was dying
I had to get out!

(*Music [11].)*

The first year we moved into the unincorporated area
called Cerro Vista Acres there was a fire.
Santa Ana winds blew someone's campfire into the
massive parched oaks and eucalyptus trees
Fire tore across regional parks flew up into the hills
where we lived
Dad waking me in the middle of the night
Me so sleepy he had to carry me through the dark
house.
Mom throwing photo albums, birth certificates,
ashtrays, World Book Encyclopedias, whatever she
could carry into a cardboard box.
We got to the car and the street was a surreal movie
All our neighbors driving by in their packed cars
everyone in pj's like us.
Horses trotting in and out of the dark

They were so beautiful and afraid
Horse-crazy me wanting to catch and ride them
bareback, one by one in the dark.
All that freedom and fear
What will happen to them?
Where will they go?
They'll come back, my dad says. They know where
home is.
Down the road pigs and goats wandering on people's
porches
All of it made magical by the flakes of white ash falling
from the night
I'm telling you this for a reason.

After the fire scare we had regular drills at our house.
Being on the upper floor of an old shake-roof home my
Dad thought we should have an alternate escape route.
Dad installed rope ladders in the gabled window seats
in our bedroom.
Very handy for a quick getaway
Which is exactly what I needed.
He never did get around to showing us just how you
escape using a rope ladder.

The Favorite sidled in as I was pulling the rope out of
the window seat.

THE FAVORITE. We had Sloppy Joe's for dinner. I
brought you some. You're welcome.
You can't sneak out the window, dork.

THE GIRL. Why, are you going to rag on me?

THE FAVORITE. I'm sorry.

THE GIRL. That I got grounded? That I got whipped
because of doing something *for you*?

THE FAVORITE. You've never gone down that rope,
you don't know how.

THE GIRL. Maybe if you yell louder dad will come up and show me.

THE FAVORITE. I'm not kidding I'll tell.

THE GIRL. *So will I.*

(*A brief intense sister-to-sister staredown.*)

THE FAVORITE. He hasn't called me. I don't know what's going on with him.

THE GIRL. Um, he's married?

THE FAVORITE. He can't stand his wife it's awful. She doesn't *understand* him. He's going to divorce her, he has to wait for the right time to tell her.

THE GIRL. Interesting.

THE FAVORITE. It's sad. I feel bad for him.

THE GIRL. Oh my god Carrie-Ann.

THE FAVORITE. You don't know everything.

THE GIRL. He's a jerk, you're an idiot that much I know.

THE FAVORITE. You don't know. It's just so messed up. I wish you understood. How he makes me feel. How nice he is. How I can tell him anything and he doesn't criticize or make fun or judge me. He makes me feel smart. Unlike *some* people.

THE GIRL. Well that's just stupid.

THE FAVORITE. Because you don't understand and you might *never* understand and I feel sorry for you. I wish you knew what it's like.

I wish I knew what it was like, I thought.

THE FAVORITE. I wish he would call.

(*Consoling, sort of.*)

THE GIRL. It's okay. He's probably just busy.

THE FAVORITE. You think?

The rope ladder was more rope than ladder.
I was pretty confident The Favorite was right
They'd find my broken corpse on the driveway in the morning.
The thing is there weren't a lot of options.

THE GIRL. Make yourself useful Carrie-Ann, hold the window up. *Higher,* I'm not a *lizard.*

She holds it up
I feed the rope out the window.
Soon enough the end that's bolted to the window seat is good and tight.

THE GIRL. Okay wish me luck.

THE FAVORITE. Good luck you're going to die.

I crawl out the window onto the roof terrified.

THE FAVORITE. Don't look down whatever you do.

THE GIRL. *Shut up.*

THE FAVORITE. I can't watch.

Bracing against the house with every body part
I inch my torso
Fraction by fraction towards the dangling "ladder"
Belly to rooftop lowering my feet then legs then hips
Okay
Little splinters of shake roof piercing my thigh flesh
Okay

(*Loud whisper.*)

THE GIRL. Are you there? *Carrie-Ann?*

THE FAVORITE. Should I get Dad?

THE GIRL. No no! Just tell me if anyone is coming upstairs.

I'm stupid, I shouldn't, I'm going to break my neck
But I can't stop myself
I can't go back
That's a kind of death.
I slide off the roof holding onto the rope for life
I snake my searching legs through the dark
Around the rope
Clutching the knots like stolen gems
Okay.

THE FAVORITE. I mean it I can't watch!

THE GIRL. Sssh! Just tell me if they're coming.

The window shuts.

Carrie-Ann?
Shit!
I worm my way down the rope

A prayer for each knot
for every second I don't fall to a gory death. Would
they even care?
I see the glow of the TV as I shinny down past the
living room
My mother's head bobbing in silent silhouette
Trying to stay awake.
Okay
I pass the broken hall window
The kitchen where The Favorite pads with a bowl of
Neapolitan ice cream?!
The dark stairs down to my father's basement office
Where he hides from my mother.
Okay
I'm on the ground.
Alive.
Sweet freedom!

I have no idea how I'll get back into my house
But mom and dad are never going to know I'm gone
Right?

(Music [12].)

Even at this time of night Zabby's house is a menagerie.
They have seven Bull Mastiffs, two Great Danes, a
Doberman Pincher, and a handful of little mutts
"Wall dogs" Dean calls them.

DEAN. On account of if they get in my way I kick
them against the wall. Stupid yapping mutts.

Zabby's dad was a former Mr. Universe or something
Their garage was filled with Rube Goldberg-type
contraptions that Dean worked out on every day
It was like a shiny torture chamber.
Her dad was just a flabby fifty-year old guy by then.
But Dean had plans to be a famous stunt-man. He was
going to change his name to *Dean James.*

DEAN. Get it? Get it?

SKINNY LYNNY. Get what?

DEAN. Are you girls on your period or just stupid?
James Dean was a rich good-looking movie star who
died in a high-speed car crash.

ZABBY. You're not rich or good looking but you can
die in a high-speed car crash if you want.

DEAN. Get the fuck out of here. You're stinking the
place up with your girl smell.

Dean never makes it as a stunt man
famous or otherwise.
He was an extra on a movie once.
I can't remember which one.
Anyway Dean was always working on his biceps or
washboard belly.
Don-o, the middle brother, on the other hand
He was more interested in cars than anything.
Half a dozen crappy vehicles littered their yard and he
usually had his head under one of them.
I'd walk past and he'd say hi and I'd think it was the

car talking
It was just surprising.
Anyway.
When I finally showed up at her house Zabby was
sitting cross-legged on the kitchen counter throwing
slices of bologna to whichever dog grabbed it the
fastest.
I kind of thought she and Skinny Lynny would be dead
drunk by now.

THE GIRL. What's up? Where's the party?

ZABBY. My parents got suspicious. They said the Jack
Daniels tasted watery. They locked up the bar. We
need reinforcements.

What Zabby's parents hadn't yet discovered was that
most of their hard liquor had been replaced with water,
Coca-Cola, Kool-Aid, or rubbing alcohol.

SKINNY LYNNY. Do you think they know it was us?

I asked Zabby what she thought we should do.

ZABBY. We should do the responsible thing and rip
off some booze from the liquor store to replace what
we drank.

THE GIRL. How are we supposed to do that? We can't
walk to the liquor store.

ZABBY. If we had a car.

SKINNY LYNNY. If we had a *car*.

THE GIRL. *We can't drive.*

ZABBY. If we had a car we could.

SKINNY LYNNY. We could.

THE GIRL. That's crazy. You're both crazy.

(*Music [13].*)

This is a good time to tell you that I had a really bad crush on Don-o.
I never told *anyone* that so you can't say *anything*.
So okay Don-o.
He was a little insane
Not like deranged but nutty.
He had this secret glee, as if he had just put a potato in someone's tail pipe and was waiting for it to blow.
You know gleeful?
He was kinder than mean Dean
And more appealing in every way
Everything about him was better
Except he had a girlfriend
Tina White.

      (She makes a sour face.)

But he always said hi to me
And he would give me The Look.

Like "I can't say anything 'cause I'm in a stupid relationship but I think you're probably someone special"
That kind of look.
So I kept my feelings to myself
For the time being.

Here he comes.

DON-O. How am I supposed to work on cars without tools? Have you seen Dean-the-dick? He hid my tool chest.

ZABBY. Hey Don-o.

DON-O. What are you girls up to?

ZABBY. Nothing.

SKINNY LYNNY. Nothing.

THE GIRL. Hi.

ZABBY. Don-o can you do us a solid?

DON-O. No more money Zabby, you already owe me twenty bucks.

ZABBY. Not money.

SKINNY LYNNY. Yeah, not money.

ZABBY. We need a car.

    (**DON-O** *laughs.*)

DON-O. A car. Are you kidding?

    (**ZABBY** *laughs.*)

ZABBY. Yeah no I'm not kidding.

SKINNY LYNNY. Do any of your, like...

DON-O. Cars in the yard?

SKINNY LYNNY. Do they actually work?

DON-O. Do you know how to drive?

SKINNY LYNNY. No.

THE GIRL. I do.

I flat-out lied.

DON-O. Yeah? Stick?

THE GIRL. No not a stick no.

DON-O. Just automatic?

THE GIRL. Pretty much yeah just automatic.

DON-O. Too bad. Mine are all manual.

He's giving me The Look.
Time slows way down
I wish everyone was gone but me and Don-o in one of his stick shifts
I wish Tina White would die peacefully in her sleep.

DON-O. But Dean's car.

ZABBY. What about Dean's car?

Dean's is an automatic says Don-o.
And Zabby says yeah but.
He's not using it says Don-o.

SKINNY LYNNY. Wait Dean's car?

I know where he hides the key says Don-o

THE GIRL. Where's Dean?

DON-O. Fucker's out. Just be back before he is. You said you could drive.

THE GIRL. *Dean's* car?

ZABBY. He would kill us.

SKINNY LYNNY. He would kill us 'til we were dead.

It's a scientific fact
The frontal lobes – the part of the brain involved in decision-making and insight
They aren't fully connected until you're in your twenties
So the adolescent brain isn't completely formed, particularly in the regions that govern impulse control, risk assessment, and moral reasoning.
This explains why I said what I said.

THE GIRL. *Let's drive.*

(*Music [14].*)

I crawl in the passenger side because remember the driver's door is busted
I scoot across the wide bench
Don-o climbs in after me
And just like that I'm sitting next to him
My hands on the wheel, nearer to him than I've ever been
Except in my teenage dreams.

Why do I feel like I'm naked?
I keep looking at my clothes to make sure they're on.

    (Music [15].)

DON-O. So.

THE GIRL. Um.

DON-O. What do you want to do?

He's giving me The Look.
I'm trying to hold in my sweat.

THE GIRL. I don't know. Just. Um.

DON-O. You know how to drive right?

THE GIRL. Oh. Yeah.

Stupid.

Where's the place where you poke in the key?

DON-O. The ignition's on the other side.

THE GIRL. Oh. I'm left-handed so everything always
seems backwards.

DON-O. I'm left-handed.

THE GIRL. Hey twins.

So stupid.

DON-O. Do you want the seat forward?

THE GIRL. No.

DON-O. So your feet touch the pedals?

THE GIRL. I mean sure. Where's the

But Don-o is
He's leaning into me.
He's
Not talking
Reaching

No
Pressing
Against me.
Oh my god
This is happening
It's happening
I'm
Holding my breath
Do it do it do it
A boy has never touched me, you know, there
Or anywhere
Oh god.
Relax
I close my eyes
Breathe
I open my legs.
He reaches

Suddenly
Don-o releases a lever, the seat jerks forward, and I am
thrust toward the windshield.
Oh.
I'm face to face with the wheel.

DON-O. You're set. Have fun. Be good.

The passenger door slams
Just like that he is gone.
And we are driving.

(*Music [16].*)

I am driving!

THE GIRL. Dear god holy shit. Okay shut up!

Zabby and Skinny Lynny shouting directions and
encouragement
The car seems too big the seats too deep.
We drive down the street
Down the boulevard on our way to

THE GIRL. Where are we going?

SKINNY LYNNY. Tastee Freeze!

ZABBY. Not Tastee Freeze. First the liquor store.

THE GIRL. Just tell me where to turn.

SKINNY LYNNY. Here turn here

ZABBY. No keep going

THE GIRL. You guys

SKINNY LYNNY. You almost hit that policeman!

THE GIRL. What policeman?

ZABBY. She's kidding.

SKINNY LYNNY. Turn the radio on!

THE GIRL. Where are we going? Which way?

ZABBY. Turn here turn here.

(Music [17].)

SKINNY LYNNY. I love this song!

We are powered by fear and guile and a contact high
and it feels amazing
The freedom, the power, the electric surge.
The world has cracked open for us this night
and we will never be thirteen again!

*(****THE GIRL*** rocks to the music.)*

Miraculously no one dies
Except the car.

ZABBY. Piece of shit car!

We've gone less than five miles and we are screwed.

THE GIRL. Great now what do we do?

SKINNY LYNNY. Walk to Tastee Freeze?

ZABBY. We're not going to Tastee Freeze, Lynny! Dean's going to kill me. He's going to kill me.

Maybe Don-o can fix it before Dean kills you I say.
Maybe Don-o will confess his love for me.
Anyway
We start walking
Off the beaten path in a rural suburb of the suburbs
Dead quiet and pitch black.

SKINNY LYNNY. You guys if we walk over the hills it's shorter you guys.

THE GIRL. No way we'd have to cut across Morningstar.

SKINNY LYNNY. Who cares it's faster.

THE GIRL. It's *trespassing* Lynny.

ZABBY. I heard they have an electrified fence.

THE GIRL. I heard that too.

SKINNY LYNNY. Electrified? Like we would be fried?

Morningstar is Morningstar Ranch a low-end horse boarding property notorious mainly because we've never actually been there
We've only heard about it.
So there's stories
The kind you make up about the shuttered house at the end of the street?
Only Morningstar is at the end of nothing.

THE GIRL. What are you doing Lynny?

She's running straight at the barbed-wire fence.

ZABBY. Lynny!

SKINNY LYNNY. You guys it's not electrified. Hey look I'm bleeding.

This does not seem like a good plan to me.

THE GIRL. What if they catch us on their property?

They're not going to catch us, climb through says
Zabby
She holds the wires up.
I climb through.

SKINNY LYNNY. Where are the horses?

ZABBY. We don't have time nut-head.

SKINNY LYNNY. Look look!

Skinny Lynny's jumping up and down.

THE GIRL. Sssh!

SKINNY LYNNY. *(Whisper.)* They're pretty.

ZABBY. *(Whisper.)* Ride one. I dare you.

No way I say. They're probably wild.

SKINNY LYNNY. They're looking at us. What can we
give them?

ZABBY. We have to get the car fixed before Dean kills
us. Come on, let's go.

THE GIRL. Let's go Lynny.

But Skinny Lynny has pulled up a fistful of grass and is
running across the pasture straight at a bunch of dark
horses.

SKINNY LYNNY. Here horsies!

THE GIRL. *(Whisper.)* Shut up!

ZABBY. *(Laughing.)* Lynny you idiot!

THE GIRL. She's nuts.

I run after her light-footed
Laughing
a sprite, a unicorn
Cantering across the dirt and grass
But I can't see Skinny Lynny.

(Loud whisper.) Lynny?

No answer, bad sign.
Where is she?

Lynny?

SKINNY LYNNY. I tripped.

Over what? I say.
Silence.

ZABBY. Lynny come on, cut it out.

THE GIRL. Are you okay?
Silence.

ZABBY. Quit messing around Lynny, we gotta go.

Then Skinny Lynny screams.
She screams so loud it sounds like a slasher movie.
She's gotta be faking it.

THE GIRL. Lynny what the hell?

ZABBY. Lynny you idiot they're gonna find us!

Then we're on the ground, fallen beside our cowering
friend.
All of us tripped over it.

ZABBY. What is that?

SKINNY LYNNY. A horse. A dead horse.

THE GIRL. No no no.

Bloated stiff stinking
a few days gone
A cougar attack, an accident, it happens.
But this.
This is different.
The horse's front legs are bound at the fetlocks by wire.
You don't do that unless you're trying to keep it from
moving

And you *never* use wire.
This was no accident.

They killed it.

SKINNY LYNNY. Why? Why kill a horse? Who does that?

ZABBY. That's sick.

SKINNY LYNNY. Poor horsie.

ZABBY. Stop looking at it.

THE GIRL. He's looking at me.

SKINNY LYNNY. He's laying there staring at us like a dead horse. *A horse with no name.*

ZABBY. We should get out of here. We should run like hell.

We get up but now a strange thing is happening.
Some of the other horses are coming over
They form a circle around us, twenty pair of sullen brown eyes.
Beautiful breathing beasts calmly staring us down
Witnesses
They know we know.

ZABBY. Come on let's go.

THE GIRL. No. We can't leave them.

ZABBY. What are you even talking about?

THE GIRL. I don't know, I want to
catch them and get them out of here.

SKINNY LYNNY. What? Wait how?

THE GIRL. I don't know, just go up to them like

> (**THE GIRL** *puts out an open palm and takes a few steps forward.*)

But they're smart horses
They don't trust us.
We're not going to bind their legs leave them to die but
how do they know that?
They turn
The group of them trot off into the dark.

(Music [18].)

We sing it the entire two hours it takes us to walk over
the hills, through backyards and down our street, back
to Zabby's house.

DON-O. *(Laughing.)* You walked all that way? It was
probably just the fuel line.

Don-o agreed to retrieve the car
I like to think he did it because he didn't want us to
get tortured by Dean and because he secretly loved me.
He charged us twenty bucks that we didn't have.

I run home
Crawl through the broken hall window just before
dawn
House is quiet
Still.
Good.
I drink Sparkletts from a Dixie cup.
Upstairs I throw my filthy self on my bed
I'm beat, my heart hurts
And crap we didn't replace the liquor!
But I can't stop thinking about that dead horse
Bloated and stiff, its legs wired together
How it must have struggled before it died
Separated from the others.
Helpless and bound
All it was trying to do was break away.

We have a new mission in life:
Save the Morningstar horses.
Then my bedroom door swings open.

MOTHER. Where in god's name have you been missy?

THE GIRL. *Mom! Hello, privacy?*

MOTHER. You could have been dead. You could be lying dead in the road right now.

THE GIRL. I'm not, sorry.

THE MOTHER. You could have been killed or raped. Or mutilated.

THE GIRL. I'm sorry Mom. Sorry. Does Dad know I snuck out?

THE MOTHER. No. Your father went out.

THE GIRL. What? Where?

THE MOTHER. For ice cream, what do you think? I want to talk to you about your sister.

Oh no please no.

THE MOTHER. Does Carrie-Ann talk to you? Do you two talk?

THE GIRL. About what?

THE MOTHER. Is she alright?

Part of me wants my mom to drag it out of me
the whole ugly mess of the affair with the neighbor's son,
Carrie-Ann's increasing torment.
Not because I'm mad at The Favorite
but because nothing good can come of something that lame.
I'm scared for her. Part of me knows that telling Mom
would be the worst possible thing to do.

THE GIRL. There is something.

THE MOTHER. I knew there was something. She's upset, is she upset with me? She's upset with me.

Cataplexy is not arbitrary
A cataleptic fit hits when my mother has big
emotions
Like laughing or crying or thinking stressful thoughts.
It's like watching a heavy snowfall on a weak tree
She's standing there
Then everything just sort of bends
And then she tips over
into my arms.

(*Music [19].*)

I tuck my mother into my bed.

THE MOTHER. You didn't... The letter. It's there.

I did steal her money so it kind of evened out.

THE GIRL. You found it?

THE MOTHER. Do not climb...the window. Or...you're
grounded.

THE GIRL. I *am* grounded.

THE MOTHER. Good. Good. Night.

THE GIRL. Is Dad coming back? Mother?

THE MOTHER. Love you.

THE FAVORITE. It was disgusting what was in that
letter. I can't talk about it. I can't even think about it.

I'm in the Favorite's bed next morning
Mom is still asleep in my bed
Dad is nowhere to be seen.

THE GIRL. You found the letter in her scarf drawer?

THE FAVORITE. He wrote all this stuff he was going to
do to Mom. It was *worse* than disgusting.

THE GIRL. You mean like torture?

THE FAVORITE. Like *sexually*. To her. On her. With her. With his finger, his tongue, his toes, everything you can think of.

THE GIRL. Oh god.

THE FAVORITE. In graphic detail like a freaky sex pamphlet. So disturbing.

THE GIRL. Who is he?

THE FAVORITE. He wrote that he wants her to use a *dildo* – on him!

THE GIRL. *Oh god*

What's a dildo?

THE FAVORITE. I can't even think about it.

THE GIRL. Why is mom getting letters from this guy?

THE FAVORITE. I can't tell you.

THE GIRL. Did she tell you?

Her, silence.

Everyone in this house is sleeping around and I haven't even been *kissed* yet!

THE FAVORITE. His name is George.

THE GIRL. I hate that name. I hate George!

THE FAVORITE. You don't even know him.

THE GIRL. I know I'd hate him.

THE FAVORITE. I met him.

THE GIRL. *You met George?*

THE FAVORITE. Well at the time I didn't know I was actually meeting him.

THE GIRL. Spill it Carrie-Ann.

(**CARRIE-ANN** *does a I Will Tell You This But Only At Great Emotional Cost to Myself face.*)

THE FAVORITE. So. Okay remember that day when we had a half-day because Willy Peaker set off fireworks which he built in chemistry class?

THE GIRL. *Yes?*

THE FAVORITE. So. Okay remember the front door was locked when we got home that afternoon because we got home early and we thought Oh mom doesn't know school is out, that's why it's locked? And mom was all like surprised and confused and "you girls aren't supposed to be home I guess I fell asleep."

THE GIRL. What the hell Carrie-Ann?

THE FAVORITE. So. Remember you were in the kitchen with Mom getting a Scooter-Pie or Ho-Ho?

THE GIRL. *Carrie-Ann.*

THE FAVORITE. So I went upstairs kind of sneaking because I wanted to wear those fringy boots of hers and I knew she wouldn't let me because of the high heels, so I didn't ask. I just went up there. She didn't know or she would have stopped me. I wish she would have stopped me. I wish wish I could un-see what I saw that day.

(**CARRIE-ANN** *does a dramatic look of mortification.*)

THE GIRL. *What did you see?*

THE FAVORITE. So.
I went into Mom and Dad's bedroom, into the closet and reached down...and where the fringy boots should have been? There was a pair of bare feet. Hairy. Bare. Man feet.
I will never forget it. For a second I didn't understand.

Then I screamed. He jumped out of the closet, no
clothes on nothing. That's how I met him.
That's how I met George. Only I didn't know it was
George.

THE GIRL. Who did you think he was?

THE FAVORITE. Mom said he was a *streaker*.

THE GIRL. *In her closet?*

THE FAVORITE. She said he was running down the
street and ran into the house to hide from the police.
At the time I believed her.

THE GIRL. That's messed up Carrie-Ann.

THE FAVORITE. It was George. When I found the
letter in her scarf drawer I knew for sure.

THE GIRL. God she is such a liar. Do you think Dad
knows?

THE FAVORITE. We can't say anything.

Considering her own situation, I could see why Carrie-
Ann had that opinion.

THE GIRL. Hey, have you heard from the jerk?

Her, silence.

THE GIRL. What's going to happen, Carrie-Ann?

THE FAVORITE. She's leaving him.

THE GIRL. She's leaving who?

THE FAVORITE. Dad. Mom's been planning it for
a while. She and George. They're going to run away
together.

(*Beat.*)

THE GIRL. That means she's leaving *us*.

(*Music [20].*)

Our plan takes shape over the phone since I am still grounded:

(Various phone calls.)

ZABBY. We're going to need a bunch of halters and ropes.

THE GIRL. Like how many Zabby?

ZABBY. Like twenty or something.

SKINNY LYNNY. Twenty?

THE GIRL. That's what Zabby said.

SKINNY LYNNY. Where the heck are we supposed to get that many halters and ropes?

ZABBY. Wire cutters, gloves, blankets.

THE GIRL. Lynny can you get a bunch of blankets?

SKINNY LYNNY. I think so. Probably. I don't know. MOM?

ZABBY. Buckets. Apples. Carrots.

SKINNY LYNNY. DO WE HAVE ANY BLANKETS WE DON'T NEED?

THE GIRL. When are we gonna do this?

DON-O. So what are you doing?

(Music [21].)

Sometimes Don-o answers when I call Zabby.

THE GIRL. We're going to catch the horses at Morningstar and I think my mom is dating this guy and I *know* my sister is and my dad might move out.

I talk too much too fast but he listens. I could be on the phone with him forever, even when we're not saying anything. Just breathing.

(*Music [22].*)

Finally
It is the big night.
We are going to save them
Save the Morningstar horses.
Zabby, Skinny Lynny, and me are going to the movies
but not *really* going to the movies
To see a Mel Brooks double-feature
Blazing Saddles and *Young Frankenstein*
We've already seen both of them like five times
We can recite things pretty much verbatim
if questioned.

Along with some lipstick-pink floral sheets
But no blankets
Skinny Lynny has brought Tupperware containers of
bourbon from her parents' stash and Boone's Farm
Blackberry Ridge that her underage brother bought
from the blind guy who works at the liquor store on
Wednesdays.

ZABBY. Totally bitchin.

Zabby takes the first slug then hands it to me.

DEAN. What are you little ladies planning on doing
tonight?

Mean Dean has snaked his way into Zabby's room
He's in my face repulsive as he is handsome.

DEAN. Hey Squirt what have you got there?

I look at the Tupperware of bourbon.

THE GIRL. Nothing.

SKINNY LYNNY. Yeah nothing.

ZABBY. None of your ugly business. Get out of my
room.

DEAN. Better be careful Squirt. Better stay out of
trouble or Daddy might ground you again. How's your
mom's boyfriend?

That fuckwad Dean listened in on my phone calls to
Zabby
Or worse, *Don-o!*
The thought of Dean picking up the receiver like a cat-
burglar
Listening with that shit-eating grin
Makes me want to throw-up on his seriously chiselled
face.
Instead I pass the Tupperware along to Skinny Lynny
I'm not doing anything I say.

What about you Toothpick? Exciting plans for tonight?

Just shine him on, Zabby says.

Skinny Lynny stares at something fascinating on the
ceiling.

DEAN. Hey Zabby, you little ladies need a *ride*
anywhere?

ZABBY. *No.*

DEAN. Not even to the movies. Or *Morningstar?*

What???

DEAN. I've got a car.

(**DEAN** *grins maliciously.*)

He knows.

ZABBY. *(Whispering.)* Fucker knows.

SKINNY LYNNY. *(Whispering.)* Oh no he knows now
what?

ZABBY. Sssh! Okay Dean. What do you want?

DEAN. Oh I don't know, maybe...

And then.
And then.
And then it got weird.
Dean points.

THE GIRL. What me? What for?

DEAN. Oh come on. What's the matter Squirt, you afraid?

THE GIRL. No way Dean I'm not afraid of you.

ZABBY. Dream on Dean, you're not doing anything to her.

DEAN. I guess you're not going anywhere.

ZABBY. Try to stop us asswipe.

DEAN. I don't think the parents will fully appreciate what you girls are planning to do.

THE GIRL. You wouldn't tell on us.

Dean does a slow smile.

SKINNY LYNNY. *He'd blow our cover!*

You know what Dean says Zabby. You know what?

DEAN. No what?

ZABBY. You're a cock-sucking bastard prick.

DEAN. Yeah? So?

ZABBY. Forget it we're not doing it then.

THE GIRL. *Wait.*

I couldn't believe it was *my mouth* that said that.
Just wait.
Zabby and Skinny Lynny are looking at me like

> (**ZABBY** *and Lynny does a 'what???' face.*)

I couldn't explain that the dead horse followed me around every night
stumbling falling on me suffocating dying slowly
its wire-tied legs churning against me.
That no matter how hard I kicked
I couldn't get out from under it.

That Morningstar was everything unfair and ugly.
That those unlucky mute horses were worth
something. That I needed to break away.
That the night was bigger than Dean.
It's okay Zabby. It's cool.

ZABBY. That's bogus, you're not going with him.

DEAN. She wants to Zab, she's a big girl.

ZABBY. Tough balls, shut up Dean!

Dean instantly pulls Zabby by the hair
His big hand grabbing it in a tight wad.

> (**ZABBY** *flinches and holds her hands
> protectively against her head.*)

DEAN. Are you saying something? Hmmm? Are you
talking?!

ZABBY. Let go motherfucker!

DEAN. I can't hear you.

Dean shoving Zabby's head down onto the table
Pinning her down
Dean knocking her head against the table.

DEAN. Now try again. Try saying something I want to
hear. Something nice.

Zabby kicking, shouting

THE GIRL. Stop! I said okay! *It's okay.*

Dean stopping.

DEAN. I like the sound of that. See how easy that was?

Zabby looking at me red-faced.

THE GIRL. It's okay Zabby.

Two minutes, she says to Dean.

DEAN. Ten.

ZABBY. *Five*. And I swear to god

THE GIRL. Just wait Zabby, okay?

Outside says Dean, *they have to wait outside.*

Zabby snarls, then stalks out of the house.

Skinny Lynny gives me a pitiful look and drops the pink sheets at my feet.

SKINNY LYNNY. They're clean. Kind of.

Then it's just me
And Dean closing the bedroom door.
He bares his big teeth in an obnoxious Mean Dean smile.

DEAN. I've been waiting for this for a long time Squirt. I think you knew that didn't you? Yeah you did. Sweet little bitch.

My fingers are stuck together
I keep swallowing my spit
That's when he makes his move
Clamp!
His mouth is huge over mine, his lips are hard, his tongue is surprisingly pointy and fills my mouth.
I don't know what to do, how to breathe
Why do people like this?

I stop thinking, stop feeling
I'm hovering, watching me pretend to know what's happening.
He digs in with his forklift tongue gouging out my mouth.
It's wrong I'm doing it wrong
I'm a terrible kisser.
I hang in, hang on
Dean eyes squeezed shut
I'm being gulped, inhaled
Him breathing hard through his nose

Then
I start to feel something
Not pleasure but
Hunger.
I don't like Dean but
I like this
I like kissing.

（*Music [23].*）

He moans, touches my breast
Oh my god
It's the weirdest thing
It feels so good and so stupid
My laugh gets muffled inside his mouth.

DEAN. What? What?

THE GIRL. Nothing just.

DEAN. Haven't you ever been felt up? Huh?

I watch him feel me up
Pressing, squeezing, rubbing
First one boob and then the other.

（*She observes herself being felt up.*）

It's okay I guess

But I want to kiss
I clamp my mouth onto his
My tongue snaking his lips open
It feels like a slip 'n' slide in there.
He moans and I realize
I'm not a bad kisser
I'm a *good* kisser.
Oh my god *Dean* is the bad kisser that's what!
How am I going to tell him that I love his brother not
him
That I'm just using him for kissing practice.
I'm starting to feel sorry for him.

It's hard to make-out with someone when you feel
sorry for them.

Zabby and Lynny are banging on the door

   ZABBY. Okay Spaz time's up.

Zabby shoves her way in

   ZABBY. Time's up Dean I'm not kidding!

   DEAN. Okay! She's ugly and doesn't know how to kiss
anyway.

You're pathetic, is what I'm thinking
But I don't say it
Tonight is bigger than Dean.

      (Music [24].)

It's after midnight.
Don-o promised to drive us to Morningstar in one of
his crap cars for another twenty dollars that we don't
have.
If this is going to happen tonight is the night
but Don-o is nowhere.

   SKINNY LYNNY. I couldn't find very many halters.

   ZABBY. Okay how many Lynny?

None she says.

Shit Lynny. What about ropes we gotta have ropes.

I say I've got four.
How are we gonna lead all those horses?

   ZABBY. I guess we're gonna lead *four* horses because
that's how many ropes we have.

   SKINNY LYNNY. Where is Don-o anyway?

   ZABBY. Probably in a fight with his girlfriend.

   SKINNY LYNNY. I wouldn't want to fight with Tina
White. Tina's mean to the max.

ZABBY. She could totally beat him up. Did you bring gloves?

SKINNY LYNNY. I have a pair of Playtex rubber gloves. See, they're yellow.

ZABBY. *Playtex?*

SKINNY LYNNY. Rubber will keep us from getting electrocuted, just in case.

All of a sudden we're in headlights
A car is slowing down
I have a feeling
It's him, it's Don-o, it's him.
I try to just be cool not stupid
but everything in me is fizzy

THE GIRL. Hi Hey.

He doesn't look up doesn't say anything.
And Zabby says "Nice of you to show up, Don - "

DON-O. I'm going home. I'm beat.

ZABBY. What about driving us?

DON-O. Not tonight kiddo. Sorry.

ZABBY. You're too tired to drive us five miles? Why, 'cause you're a dick?

DON-O. Maybe. Maybe I am a dick.

You are a dick says Zabby.

He doesn't take the bait, just stares at his steering wheel.

ZABBY. You definitely are Don-o.

THE GIRL. Zabby forget it, we can walk.

ZABBY. Yeah he has enough energy to hump his girlfriend all night but not enough to do what he *promised.*

DON-O. Look I said I'm sorry.

ZABBY. Great, why don't you go fuck yourself, dick?

Zabby throws the Playtex gloves at her brother.

ZABBY. We're walking all the way to Morningstar because my brother is a *dick*.

She stalks off into the dark.
Skinny Lynny waits a minute, grabs the gloves, goes.
I'm standing alone in the headlights.

THE GIRL. Hey it's totally cool if you don't take us.

Don-o finally looks up, his eyes round, soft.
He's looking at me like
He's looking at me.

DON-O. Do you know how amazing you are?

This is it
This is the night
He's looking at me
Tina's pregnant he says
He stares at the steering wheel.

Oh.

That's it.
He drives away slowly
Leaves me in the dark.

> *(Music [25].)*

The girl who won the contest that summer
She was from Bakersfield.
I didn't know they even had horses in Bakersfield.
"Amirage," that was the winning name
Amirage.

> *(Beat.)*

It's a really good name.

We're walking and walking, but I don't know anymore
It seems like a stupid idea now
Saving horses saving anything.
Thinking Don-o was a possibility when all the time he
was just something I made up.
But right then we were there
We were at Morningstar
With our ropes and our rubber gloves and our plan
Our really stupid plan.

>   *(Urgent whisper.)*

  THE GIRL. You guys wait a minute. Wait a minute.

Starlight falling on the hills so it looks like a dark day
not night
Too bright, too easy to see.
But we are cutting the unelectrified barbed wire
Walking through
Skinny Lynny somehow managing to get her hair
caught on the barbs.

>   *(Whispered.)*

  THE GIRL. Wait you guys!

Walking softly, clucking and cooing
Holding out carrots and apples
Here horsie

>   *(Clucking.)*

>   *(Whispered.)*

Sssh!
A couple of horses trot away.

>   *(Whispered.)*

Go slow.

>   *(Clucking.)*

ZABBY. Come on, come here horse.

Zabby slips a rope over the neck of a mangy bay mare
Skinny Lynny stalks a zippered buckskin and a greedy
palomino
I stand there.
*What are we doing? What does it matter? We can't save
them all.*
Warm breath on my neck my ears
It would feel nice if it weren't a horse and I wasn't
scared.

THE GIRL. You guys look!

Ssshhh!
An appaloosa
Young, probably green, but super friendly
She likes me, I don't know why
I don't have any carrots.
She's nuzzling
Aw
Super sweet.

SKINNY LYNNY. Whoa whoa whoa!

Skinny Lynny is kind of being led by the buckskin and
the palomino.
Zabby is trying to make the bay move.
The appaloosa lets me pet her
I put the rope around her –

(**THE GIRL** *looks underneath for confirmation.*)

His
His neck.
Smooth and shiny grey with light spots.
He walks with me like we've been doing this forever
Like we were meant to be.
We start up the hill
Away from Morningstar.
We are doing this, we are saving these horses!
Not doing something wrong but making something
right.

Oh crap they're coming says Zabby.

SKINNY LYNNY. What, no way who?

We don't know who or what but they are in a truck
They are driving across the dark dirt pasture straight
at us.

ZABBY. Giddy-up, come on let's go, let's book!
Her horse is a statue.

ZABBY. Oh forget it.
She looses her horse and slaps its rump with the rope.

ZABBY. Run away, be free you idiot!

The mangey bay just stands there. Why doesn't she
want to be free? What are we doing? I can't think.

Skinny Lynny's horses are dancing around
Yanking her long arms.

SKINNY LYNNY. Hey hey, you stop that. I'm taking
you to a better place so back off.

Her horses aren't interested in going anywhere but
back to Morningstar, they drag her down the hill
through cactus towards the coming truck
Crazy Lynny, she's crying, swearing
Zabby is like let go, let go, let go they're gonna kill you!
Finally finally Skinny Lynny releases her death grip
Her horses fly away.
Ropes and tails trailing behind them

        (Clucking.)

Come on
Me and my Appy start trotting up the hill
Faster, faster come on!
We have a headstart they won't follow they can't
Stupid truck doesn't fit through the fence
But they jump out of their truck and start running
Fuckity-fuck.

ZABBY. Shine it, let's get out of here!

THE GIRL. No way Zabby, I'm not letting go.

(Clucking.)

The men are yelling something about jail and our
asses
Zabby and Lynny are screaming
What are you doing?

I don't know.

I didn't know that night that my sister would swallow
a bottle of pills
Pills that she stole from her married boyfriend's
mother I didn't know.

(Clucking.)

I keep running, running
Out of breath, out of my mind.
I didn't know that night my mom would be waiting for
George to pick her up
Take her away.
I didn't know.

(Clucking.)

They're closing the distance, those guys are fast.
Come on, come on! There's no way I think
Then I rethink.
Whoa!
I stop the appy.
What are you doing?
I climb onto his back
His shiny slippery strong back.
I wrap my hands in his wiry grey-black-white mane
Like my mom's hair when she doesn't dye it
I lean against his neck, squeeze, my legs hold on.

(**THE GIRL** *rides.*)

It's happening
We are running, running
Starlight falling on the hills
Hope riding fear
Running free
It's happening.

Zabby and Lynny scatter shouting
Keep going you're almost there, almost!
Zabby on the hillside
Her arms overhead screaming
Go go go!
And then what?
We keep running
And then what?

In three weeks Skinny Lynny will go to the doctor to
have infected cactus quills removed from her belly.
She'll move to a four hundred-acre ranch in Northern
California where she'll have horses
She'll break her neck riding one
I'll never see her again.

The house is lit up when I get home
It's not even daylight and I'm already busted.
I'm filthy
Covered in horse hair and dried blood
There's nothing I can say or do
I am dead.
The house is quiet inside
My mom is awake
More awake than I've seen her in the middle of the
day.
She's watching The Favorite who's asleep on the couch.

THE MOTHER. They had to give her something to
make her throw up, get the pills out, says my mother.
She's alright. I don't know why. Why would she take so
many pills? Does she talk to you? Do you and Carrie-
Ann talk?

I sit next to her
Mom leans her head on my shoulder
We look at Carrie-Ann asleep.

THE MOTHER. Did Carrie-Ann tell you about George?

THE GIRL. God Mom.

THE MOTHER. He got bad news. Very bad news. Cancer. Fast-growing, terminal.

THE GIRL. Oh.

THE MOTHER. He has maybe two months to live.

THE GIRL. That's fast.

THE MOTHER. He said. He said he just couldn't do that to me.

THE GIRL. I look at her. I can see it, the desperation. Would you, mom? Would you leave us?

Her, silence.

THE MOTHER. Missy you could have been dead. In the road. You could be dead and I'd be sitting here.

THE GIRL. I'm not dead. I stole a horse. The owners at Morningstar caught me and called the police. I think they're pressing charges.

THE MOTHER. *Why?*

THE GIRL. Mom *it's illegal*.

THE MOTHER. Why did you steal a horse? Tonight of all nights?

In six months when she's out shopping my mother will run into George. He'll be with another woman.
He won't have a lot to say.

My dad comes up from the basement.
I offer to get The Belt but he shakes his head no
Goes back to the basement.
Okay.
I'm here.

(Music [26].)

The Morningstar people never did press charges. They knew that we knew about the dead horse, the horse with no name.
They said it had been "inadvertently hobbled."
Whatever. They closed down within a year. I like to think we had something to do with that.
That summer we knew what we'd been through was something real. Something that changed everything.
We weren't freedom fighters, we were *freedom takers*
Clutching fistfuls of it like thieves of air
Like starved spirits.
That's how I remember it.
That summer we made a pact to no matter what, meet at Tastee Freeze every ten years.

> **(THE WOMAN** *looks around.)*

It's not a Tastee Freeze anymore, but I keep coming back
Keep thinking that...
Right after high school Zabby got married, got religion. We lost touch. I guess she's still married, still loves Jesus.
She might even be the mother of teens, like me.
Corruption fodder.
Irreverent, erupting
Scarching and stealing
Freedom takers.

> **(THE WOMAN** *glances around the room, nods to the audience, maybe even lifts a glass – "that happened," then exits.)*
>
> *(Music continues.)*

End of Play